Tales from the Canyons of the Damned

DANIEL ARTHUR SMITH

Tales from the Canyons of the Damned No. 18

First Edition

Special thanks to Jessica West

ISBN-13: 978-1946777331 ISBN-10: 1946777331

Cover By Daniel Arthur Smith

Horror Fiction from Holt Smith ltd
Agroland
Tower

~×~

For Susan, Tristan, & Oliver, as all things are.

~*~

A Personal Account of the Battle of the *Eurydice* and the *Sceptre*

Kevin Lauderdale

~*~

Sedmon Hall
Buckshire
September 1, 1844

My dear son Andrew,

As I write this, you are about to matriculate into Oxford. I feel I should offer you some words of wisdom.

As you know, the Royal Navy was my university, the Admiralty Board my dons, and the sea my examining hall. I learned bravery as well as navigation under Captain Anson and thrift from his steward, Crumpton.

In the June of 1808, I was younger than you are now. Just 15 years old and a newly-minted midshipman. I was still three years away from being eligible to take the exams to see if I could pass for a lieutenant. My world was the HMS *Eurydice*, a frigate built by Hillhouse out of Bristol and launched in 1785. It was the middle of the Napoleonic Wars, and we were under general orders to "burn, sink, or capture" any enemy vessel we encountered.

The same went for the monsters.

The *Eurydice* was a 38-gun fifth-rate. On her upper deck were 26 18-pound cannons, each of those guns capable of firing their balls of solid iron a distance of 2,000 yards, though they were rarely accurate beyond half that. The quarterdeck sported eight nine-pounders, as well as four smaller, squat 18-pound carronades. She was 141 feet long and 38 feet wide at the beam, had three masts, and carried 260 men. It had taken 60 acres of oak to build her.

On the day it started, we were in the Atlantic Ocean, some 200 miles off Spain's westernmost point, Cape Finisterre. I know because Captain Anson had just taken the latitude.

For this ceremony, repeated every day at noon, he gathered us handful of midshipmen on deck with our brass sextants to do our own latitude calculations, which Himself would then check. Say what you will about the roughness of a man who started his career in the Navy as a runaway farm boy from Dorset, but Captain Anson knew his latitude from his lanyard.

Dave Shaw, a fellow middie, had just wrung the bell for noon when high overhead in the rigging, we heard the call, "Sail ho! Six points off the port!"

The captain pulled out his telescope and turned to his left. "There she is. She's flying our colours." He paused for a moment and passed the telescope to me. "Very well,

Mister Richmond, can you make her number?" Trust the captain to turn everything into a lesson. Or a test. I may have been heir to the eighth-largest fortune in England, but to the captain I was still another sniveling middie who needed to prove his worth.

I applied the telescope to my right eye. Like every ship in the Royal Navy, this newcomer flew a number of pendants and flags. From a distance, another ship might not be able to make out *Eurydice* painted in black along our stern's yellow hull. But every ship in His Majesty's Navy also had a number. Ours was 214, and it was announced by multicoloured signal flags flying from our mizzenmast.

At first, everything was just a blur until I focused the scope. The coloured designs on this newcomer's flags swam into focus and I read the code. "Two…zero…four!" I shouted, and I handed the telescope back to the captain, a proud smile on my face.

"Thus…" He looked at me expectantly.

"I… I don't know, sir."

Captain Anson shook his head disappointingly. He turned to Michael Peller, one of the other middies. "Mister Peller?"

"HMS *Emerald* sir," said Peller. The grind! The scrub! He was only a year older than me, but a full head taller. He turned to look down on me and said with a snarling smile, "It's only on the page opposite us."

We middies weren't required to have memorized all of our Navy's ships' numbers. But paging through back issues of the Navy List was Peller's idea of a pleasant afternoon. Naturally, I flipped through them myself every now and then while in the ship's head. Along with each active ship's name and number were listed her current officers and her present station. In the back of every issue were such things as the complex table of pay for the navy—Admiral of the Fleet: £1,825 a year. I remember it to this day. A princely sum even now. We midshipman barely made £30 a year—the rules for the distribution of prize-money, and dress uniform regulations. All the sorts of things that were of interest to a young man just beginning his career.

There was the sound of a single cannon shot from the *Emerald*. A welcoming signal.

"Ah, she's made us, too," said Anson. He turned to me. "Go and tell Mister Armbruster to bring us about." The Captain expectantly looked at Peller again.

"She's a thirty-six, sir," said Peller the grind. "A fifth-rate like us."

The captain thought for a moment. He was doing the complex calculations of precedence. The captain of the lesser ship always called upon the captain of the greater. But we were evenly matched.

"Oh, hell," he sighed. "I could use a change of scene. Let's go see if…" He turned to Peller.

"Captain Wallace, sir," the scrub helpfully provided.

"Captain Wallace has any news for us."

~*~

In an hour, our ships had closed ranks and were alongside each other, yardarm to yardarm. The *Emerald* and the *Eurydice* were indeed of nearly equal size and configuration, though our sister looked like she'd been chewed up and spit out by Jonah's whale itself.

Her starboard hull was scarred with cannon damage. One of her three masts was broken at the midpoint, the remaining stub bristling with inch-thick splinters. Her mizzen and main topsails hung in long shreds.

And everything was wet. The sails showed the tell-tale discolouration of dampness. Teams of men worked hard at the giant wheels of the bilge pumps while others wrung out their clothes over the side of the ship.

The two captains, myself, Peller, and two of the *Emerald*'s middies met in Captain Wallace's cabin. Wallace was a middle-aged man with black hair down to his shoulders. We were all in our blue dress uniforms. The *Emerald's* smelled musty.

Wallace began with a wave of his hands indicating the shattered glass and wood everywhere. "It was the *Sceptre*, a French ship of the line. A seventy-four."

I shuttered. That meant twice as many guns and three times as many men. A third again as long as us and at least ten feet wider at the beam.

"Out-classed and out-gunned," said Anson kindly. "You were lucky to survive at all. That you did and escaped speaks to your credit, sir. And your men."

Wallace shook his head. "We only escaped due to a providential storm." He spread out a map on the cabin's table. "Though I don't know how providential. It seems to have damaged us as much as the Frenchies did. That was yesterday afternoon. We had fixed ourselves *there* at noon." He pointed to a location about 75 miles west of our location. "Seemed like she came out of nowhere. She had the weather gauge and was on us in no time. She came up on our starboard and fired a full broadside from her lower deck." I winced. That meant all fourteen of her 36-pounders at once. "You know what they say, only one of the cannons has to get lucky. It did. Took down the foremast."

"What about your sails?" I piped up. Anson looked at me sternly. "Sorry, sir. I know it's not my place to ask, but…they looked *torn*. I mean, not with the usual holes a cannonball would make."

Captain Wallace leaned back. The oldest of his middies, a short man of about twenty-five with red hair and a full beard, said, "Aye, that was the monster."

"A monster!?" Peller all but leapt from his seat. Then it was his turn for our captain's glance of disapprobation.

"What did it look like?" Captain Anson asked. His voice was calm and measured. I was close to shaking.

Monsters! We hadn't encountered any yet, but sailors' tales spread. Tales of tentacled faces and shambling mounds with a hundred eyes. Things more animal than man, things so unholy and ugly that they were kept under canvas until battle, lest the mere sight of them drive the French crews insane. And always claws, wings, and teeth.

Some said Boney had found them in back in '98 when he had invaded Egypt. Supposedly one of his *savants* had unearthed an ancient tome. Rumor had it the thing was bound in human skin and embossed with symbols of demonic origin. It was from this book that a *philosophe* from the Académie des Sciences had conjured forth the various monsters that had started accompanying French warships about a year prior.

Wallace said, "I didn't get a good look. Seemed like right behind the *Sceptre* came the storm. There were...blurs and the rains of the storm."

The red-headed middie said, "It had wings. It could move through the pounding rain as slick as a dolphin. Its claws are what shredded the canvas."

"No doubt it would have done more, but that storm came right between us and slapped us here. If not for that storm we'd still be there. Or captured."

In general, the French shot to disable our ships from maneuvering. Take down a couple masts, or blow apart a ship's sails, then she was dead in the water and ripe for the boarding. The Royal Navy, on the other hand, sought to destroy as often as to capture. Like many a captain of that time, Anson preferred to fire our cannons into our enemies' hulls. Hence the old saw that in any sea battle French guns would be pointing up while British pointed down.

Captain Anson said, "We'll give you our spare mast. That will get you back to England or the base at Gibraltar. And then we're going after her."

Later, as we left the *Emerald*, I said, "Sir, I don't understand. The *Sceptre* has thrice our complement, and she almost demolished the *Emerald*. No one would expect that we could possibly do her any harm. Shouldn't we report her last position to the Admiralty so that they might send out a search squadron of first-rates? Why are *we* chasing after her?"

Anson turned to me. I will never forget the determined look in his eyes nor the patriotic zeal in his voice when he said to me, "It is French, this is war, and there is a monster aboard."

~*~

Sailing is an inexact science. The seas are huge; your ship is small. You aim yourself in the general direction of your quarry and hope for the best. There was none of this steam power that you have today. We were at the mercy of the wind, and, of course, our crew's ability to manipulate the sails so to capture that wind in such a way that it pushed our ship in the intended direction.

We had a top-notch crew, but the fact remains that not even the best crew, nor captain, can conjure wind out of nothing.

We were lucky to have had the wind at our back—the weather gauge, we call it. What little luck a ship could have, we had with us.

We also had Captain Anson's years of experience and understanding of French naval tactics.

"The storm blew the *Emerald* east," he said to Armbruster, his first lieutenant. The two of them stood by the ship's wheel, beginning our quest. "If I was the *Sceptre*, hunting for a smaller ship that was clearly damaged, I'd follow behind the storm and come after her."

"Bird in the hand, sir?"

"Why go looking for a new hawk when you have a crippled sparrow? But instead of finding that sparrow dead in the water, she'll find us."

"An un-crippled sparrow, sir?" asked Armbruster.

"A well-rested, well-fed, and well-armed sparrow," said the captain with a grin.

Crumpton, who was bringing the captain his tea while this conversation took place, muttered, "We're not much of a prize for them, but crikey, if we took her…I could set up my carriage." Crumpton was of old Puritan stock. He'd been baptised Wait-Still-And-The-Lord-Will-Provide Crumpton. But lest you think that he had fallen into the sin of greed, remember that, for all our talk of destruction, ideally, we wanted to capture the *Sceptre*.

French ships, at the time, were superior. They were faster and carried more guns with greater efficiency. Capturing one settled two problems: it deprived the French of a ship, and it saved us the trouble of building one. To encourage this, the government offered prize-money.

When a ship was captured and still serviceable, the Admiralty would purchase it for its approximate value. £20,000 for a frigate like ours, three times that for a first-rate ship of the line like Lord Nelson's *Victory*. Those payments were the stuff of legend. Every man aboard had done the calculations in his head a hundred times.

The distribution of the value of the ship was by eighths. The captain got two eighths (fair enough), one eighth went to the admiral who issued the ships' orders (For what?! I ask you. Sitting on his arse half a world away? Always thought that a swindle.). The rest went to the crew. Three eighths were divided among the various levels of officers, from lieutenants to warrant and petty, including midshipmen. The last two eighths went to everyone else from the able-bodied seamen to the cook and ship's boys. A small prize might be worth a sailor's year's pay. A grand capture could indeed set you up for life.

I was already set, but then there is no such thing as too much gold. As you yourself will one day learn. Particularly when you must pay taxes.

It was not yet eleven in the morning on the day after our meeting with the *Emerald* when we heard the cry of, "Sail ho!" from aloft.

"Where away?" asked the captain.

"Two points off the starboard!"

"It must be them. Even if it's not, no one's going to catch us unawares. Beat to quarters!"

"Beat to quarters!" the order was repeated, and the air filled with the thundering roll of the drums as all hands were called into battle.

"Here," said Peller, handing me a dirk. It was only 18 inches of steel, but it would suffice should we board or be boarded. I nodded and smiled at him. Were we friends? We were not enemies. We were shipmates. Despite any complaints I might have of him, we were united in a cause. "Looks like we get the joy of our toast."

I'm sure you've heard that we sailors used to toast, "Wives and Sweethearts...may they never meet." Actually, we had a different toast for each day of the week. That one was Saturday's. My favorite was always Thursday's, as a wish to clear the path of promotion: "A bloody war, or a sickly season." Today was Friday morning. We'd uttered that toast only hours earlier.

"Run up the pendant!" the captain bellowed.

Hands pulled at the rigging, and soon the tapering red-and-white flag of England, the Cross of St. George, trailed along some 50 feet from our mizzen mast's peak. There was to be no trickery, no flying of false colours to confuse the enemy at first.

Peller handed me his glass. He was a scrub, but he was always prepared. I could just make out the white of the sails across the miles. The sky was clear and blue, the sea, that proverbial shade of wine-dark. There was no storm. That, at least, put an end to the rumor that had quickly swept the ship, that the French also had a means of creating storms at will.

Armbruster asked the captain, "What are your orders, sir?"

"Get me close enough to see that monster. Then I'll decide."

"Aye, aye, sir."

An hour later, after the ceremony of the noon latitude (Standards must be maintained, or else what were we fighting for?), Captain Anson produced his glass.

"Ah, I believe I can see some...thing," he said.

I looked through my telescope.

And I saw, for the first time, a monster.

I don't know if it was an avatar of one of the *Grands Anciens*, as they called them, or perhaps one of their spawn. Andrew, no doubt you'll recall the ones we've seen stuffed and mounted at the British Museum. This one was just as ugly.

It was nearly human in form, though a giant to be sure. It stood as tall as two men, and each leg and arm were proportionally long. The arms ended in massive claws. Its muscles bulged in sharp relief, like those of a marble statue of Hercules straining against the Nemean Lion. The monster stood naked at the ship's prow. That flesh, glistening in the sun and sea spray, was the bright purple of a bishop's vestments. Its body and head were hairless. Where there should have been a face was only a huge, circular orifice lined with jagged teeth. This mouth opened and closed in a dilating spiral. There were no eyes, nor nose. But huge, bat-like ears sprouted from either side of its skull. I stared intently through the glass. Proud wings, equally bat-like, sprung up from behind the monstrosity. I adjusted my glass and brought the ship's French flag into focus. The *Sceptre*, to be sure.

"May I?" asked Dr. Wald, our ship's physician, and I handed him the scope. The Doctor grunted. "It doesn't have any eyes. Huge ears. Bat-like. Bat's wings, too."

"A rather lubberly beast," said Captain Anson, and we all laughed.

The Doctor gave the glass back to me and said, "There's an Italian cove name of Spallanzani. He has postulated that bats 'see' with their ears."

The captain snorted. "Italian."

The Doctor continued, unabated. "He thinks they see by listening to the echos of their screeches. Echos sound different if they're bouncing back from a long ways off as opposed to near. You must have noticed that in your travels." We all nodded. "Spallanzani is a Fellow of the Royal Society. I heard him give a talk in London a few months back."

"Oh, Royal Society," said the Captain with gruding respect. "Very well then."

From the corner of my eye, I saw a flash of light.

"Duck!" I yelled as I pulled Peller down. I heard a splash but felt no shock of the cannonball. We both stood up. The Doctor pointed behind us. I could see the white of the water where the ball had sunk.

"They're just getting their range," said the Captain. "Which reminds me...Darby!"

Instantly, Darby, our ten-year-old powder-boy, stood at the Captain's side, his arms full of well-stuffed flannel bags. The captain bent down and said conspiratorilly, "Darby, how are we fixed for fuses?"

"Oh, we've ever so many," the boy chirped, hefting the bags.

Darby spent half his time at the thankless chore of twisting handfuls of gunpowder into pieces of paper to fashion fuses for the cannons. The *Eurydice* had one of the best-drilled gun crews in the Royal Navy. We spent an hour a day at practice and could by now get off one shot per minute. Powder, ball, fuse...loading each of them took some time. We went through a prodigious number of cannonballs and fuses at practice. I've often wondered if there isn't a fortune to be made salvaging all that iron from the sea floor. If one could get to it.

"That's 'Captain,'" whispered Peller, not unkindly. Everyone liked Darby.

"Ever so many, *Captain*," appended Darby.

Anson smiled. "Excellent. Make sure each gun has plenty. This may take some time." Darby saluted and ran off, depositing several bags next to each of our nine-pounders.

I heard another whistle and splash. I looked over the side. "Much closer, sir," I reported.

"Then it is time we began." The captain turned from the wheel to face the deck where crew members scurried. "Men!" he called. "It is quite simply us or them. We are out-gunned and out-manned. There will be only absolute victory or defeat." He learned forward. "Want to have your sons calling you 'Monsieur'?"

"No!" came our full-throated cry.

"Want to see the Tricolour flying over Windsor Castle?"

"No!" we roared.

"Want to hear the French Disease called 'the English Disease'?"

"Nooo!" came the loudest roar of all, and we pounded our fists and stomped our feet against the hull and deck.

"Very well then. For England and King George!"

Our cheer was deafening.

"Mr. Armbruster! Bring us about!"

Armbruster spun the ship's wheel.

~*~

The *Sceptre* was aiming for us. She was turning to get to seaward and windward of the *Eurydice*, and we were pointed into the wind, where we would be most eligible to rake her with a broadside.

We had been closing in on each other slowly (that fickle wind). But now, like the last remaining grains of sand circling in an hourglass, both ships seemed to be moving faster and faster towards an inevitable meeting point.

The *Sceptre* fired. I heard the whistling of a spread of 36-pounders flying above my head. I laughed. True to form, the French had aimed too high, leaving only one hole each in our main topgallant and its staysail.

In what seemed only a moment, we shot past each other. Suddenly we were moving away, presenting only our stern—our posterior, as I liked to think of it—to the French.

It was then that they sent the monster.

I heard the high-pitched "Whee! Whee!" of its screeches. I turned and saw it alight from their quarterdeck deck.

As the creature flew closer, I learned how apt the word *monster* truly was. Everything about it was unnatural. No animal in nature is that sickly shade of purple. To see, living and moving, a mass of colour I had hitherto only seen still in pictures or as cloth fogged my mind with confusion. It was as if grapes had sprung from some painting and were charging towards me. Likewise, I had seen bats and I had seen men. The inherent wrongness of their combination filled me with dread. Who had made such a beast? Surely not God. Factor in also that it was just so damned ugly! Even the shark, for all its teeth, still has a face, with eyes and a nose. To confront—and I cannot stress this enough—a living creature that had no face nearly sent me to the ship's rails to vomit like some landlubber.

The monster cleared the distance so quickly. It hovered just above our mainmast, wings beating, insane mouth screeching and teeth grinding.

I swear I could smell it as well. There was an earthy, beastly smell that overpowered even the sea. Suddenly it occurred to me: Where was the smell of gunpowder? Why weren't we firing at it?

Of course. It was directly above us.

We couldn't aim our cannons that high. They weren't built for that many degrees of movement. For a moment, I had the fancy of unblocking a cannon, hefting it on my shoulder, and firing straight up at the monster. But even the smallest weighed hundreds of pounds.

"We need to lure it lower," said Peller. He was a scrub, but he was right. But what could lure the monster back out over the ocean and into cannon range?

A French cannonball struck us. Though it was reflected by our hull's five inches of solid oak, its force nonetheless set the ship ringing like the bell at Sedmon Chapel.

The monster screeched again, still hovering in place above us, but moving its head back and forth. It was getting its range and "looking" with sound for something. The easiest prey? The captain? Could it tell an officer from, say, a powder-boy? I ran my eyes across the deck, worried for our smallest shipmate. Darby was fine, huddled up against a cannon near Peller's feet.

Then my eye caught sight of a marine high in our clouds of sail. He had climbed to the mizzen top, 75 feet above us. His red uniform against the blue sky and white canvas brought to mind the Union Jack. He was moving through the rigging armed with a rifle. That was it! Take the battle to the monster. But the creature turned and swooped at him. Our marine fired, missed, and was set upon. I heard no scream from the man as I saw the beast fly out over the sea and drop his body. As he fell, he broke apart into two large pieces, each trailing their own pendants of red.

Now the creature was over the water instead of our deck, but still too high up for a cannon's angle. And too distant for rifle or pistol shot.

The French had stopped firing on us, obviously intending to conserve their powder and iron while the monster made short work of our sails and crew.

The creature was blind, the Doctor had said. But with those ears, sounds would also draw its attention. If I could somehow get it to swoop down close to me, then our men could shoot it with small arms.

The monster's shadow moved across the deck accompanied by more of its skin-crawling shrieks. The shadow darkened across Darby and—of course!

Bullets and cannon balls were the wrong type of weapon!

I slid to the cannon nearest me, reached down, and grabbed a handful of Darby's fuses. I was under no illusion that a finger's-length of powder would kill the monster, but that was not my plan. I lit two fuses and counted. They usually lasted three seconds before setting off a cannon. I tossed them overboard, high in the air. They described an acute arc as they fell just inches from the ship's side. The monster turned its head to follow the sound of the ensuing explosion right beside me.

I lit the remaining fuses and repeated my actions.

Just moments after the second explosion, the monster swooped down, aiming right at me.

That's when I stabbed it.

It took both of my hands forcing the dirk's hilt, but I managed to run the beast's chest clear through with my steel. I held tight, trying to steer it on deck, as if I were landing a large fish, but it broke away from me, and the sickly purple form flew from the ship.

The monster hovered off our port side for a moment. It was far from dead, and now it was angry. Its horrible vocalizations grew louder. It dipped its wings, floated gracefully over the ship's rail, and landed on deck facing me.

As it pulled my dirk from its chest, a greasy grey ichor trickled from the wound. The creature hurled my weapon at me with such strength that it pierced my left boot and foot and pinned me to the deck.

It stepped towards me. Its grinding maw had a mesmerizing effect. All I could see were teeth. All I could feel was cold.

Then I heard a panting cry of "*Eurydice!*" and turned to see Peller wielding, of all things, an anchor. One of our smaller ones, to be sure. It was as long as his chest and must have weighed 75 pounds if it weighed an ounce. He waddled across the deck, struggling mightily with it. Then, like some Scottish pole tosser, he hurled the anchor at the beast with every ounce of strength he possessed.

"Lubber!" I yelled at the monster and let myself fall to the left, dislocating my ankle. It turned to follow me, and Peller's anchor lodged itself deep in the beast's right side, half-severing that wing.

With a cheer, three of our mates fell upon the anchor's chain and pulled. The monster fell to the deck, and three more crewmen began sawing at its wings with daggers and an axe.

It was Darby—brave Darby, who lost the first joints of three fingers when he shoved an entire bag-full of his fuses, already burning, into the piteously-grinding maw of the monster—who finally did it in.

The blood never did come entirely clean from the deck no matter how hard we sanded. And I know you've met more than a dozen of old Eurydices who proudly wear one of those huge, serrated teeth as a watch fob. We're lucky none of us was killed when the head exploded and those dental horrors flew everywhere like shrapnel. Still, the Admiralty paid handsomely for the remains.

The rest, as they say, is history. Whether you wish to ascribe our success to Providence or skill, certain facts remain. We had the wind, and the French were slow to react. We boarded them and found their discipline lacking and their man-to-man combat decidedly lubberly. Perhaps they were in shock after losing their monster. Or perhaps they had relied for too long a time upon the thing softening their opponents. In an hour, their ship was ours.

Bringing the *Sceptre* in to port was one of the grandest moments in my life. The accompanying reward paid off your grandfather's estate taxes and built the Hall's east wing.

So there you have it.

The best advice at sea is also the best advice on land: Keep your steel sharp, your powder dry, and your shipmates close.

Your Father,

Richmond

~*~

Voices from the Deep
Terry R. Hill

~×~

"Oh no...we hit a whale, sir!"

"Repeat, Ensign?"

"Sir, we hit a whale. An orca just surfaced along with the debris...but not in a good way."

Six months later.
The National Oceanic and Atmospheric
Administration's (NOAA) Marine Mammal
Laboratory cetacean research facility.
Seattle, Washington: 9:38 a.m.

Dr. George Martin slowly walked around the edge of the pool en route to his desk. He ran the cetacean research facility for NOAA, and as far as government jobs, it wasn't bad. It provided adequate job security so he could actually focus on doing research rather than spending his time brownnosing and schmoozing for grants and donations, or dealing with the corporate office's bottom line. He'd gone through engineering college with his childhood friend Tom Gladwell, but shortly after entering the workforce, it was clear he'd made a terrible mistake. He went back to school to learn about these strange mammals that decided long ago to leave dry land and go back to the sea.

And, it just so happened that George had a tendency to understand dolphins and whales better than people. People, he just didn't *get*. Like his ex-wife. He loved her but never really understood her. And in time, she gave up trying to understand him. That was ten years ago and he hadn't dipped his toes into the pool of relationships again. Been there, done that, got the t-shirt.

The smell of the salt water, the humidity, and the hum of the filters, pumps, and florescent lights were comforting to George. Perhaps because they were familiar and unchanging, unlike all the other facets of his life.

A large black and white blob floating under the water slowly surfaced, blowing a spray of water into the air. Lennie hadn't noticed him yet, which wasn't entirely surprising, given his condition. The male orca, brought to him six months ago by his friend Tom, was barely responsive. It was suspected to have closed-head injuries to its fourth paralimbic lobe as a result of some military job Tom was involved with. George had learned over the years not to ask too many questions about what his friend did. But, studying the whale brain, specifically the fourth lobe, which isn't present in the human brain, was George's specialty. That was why Tom had reached out to him. Access to one that didn't function properly was hard to come by and incredibly valuable—sometimes more is learned about how something works by observing one which doesn't. George's luck changed the day Lennie unluckily encountered the U.S. Navy.

Lennie had pulled through miraculously, with no small effort by George's team and that of a few cetacean colleagues in the field. Most of them thought George was wasting his time, and even his management suggested he was carelessly throwing his funding into the pool. But all of the money and incredibly long hours paid off. Lennie was alive and had begun to respond to him. He processed information significantly slower than an orca in the wild, but at least he had stopped incessantly swimming in circles. And while he would never admit it, George had become a little attached to Lennie as well.

Of course, George had experience with perception issues and the brain; his son, Dillon, was moderately to severely autistic. Perhaps Lennie and George were a match made in heaven since there was an undeniable reoccurring theme in his life.

George chuckled to himself. Not long after it was clear the orca would survive, his new graduate student, Patrick Goby, named him Lennie. When asked why that particular name, Patrick said it was because he had recently been forced to read *Of Mice and Men* as part of his graduate studies. George's name plus the fact that the orca wasn't quite right mentally and needed someone to take care of it, Lennie was the natural choice for a name. Patrick said he figured something good should come out of him having to suffer through that book.

The pool room was quite large and well lit. He had to have a big pool because he liked to get the big boys in there to study when possible. But for now, it was just Lennie. He walked over to the water and slapped the surface to get the whale's attention.

Moments later, Lennie surfaced and exhaled a plume of water spray.

"Hello Lennie!" said George as he did every morning. Consistency was a good thing.

But this morning, Lennie replied with a series of clicks and squeals which sounded very much like George's greeting.

This is new.

It didn't sound anything like a human voice, but Lennie had nailed the intonation and pitches.

All week Lennie had been making new sounds when George arrived in the mornings, but this was something entirely different and too close to be a coincidence.

"Hello Lennie!"

A few seconds later Lennie echoed as before and even a little clearer.

Interesting.

The two approached each other toward the side of the pool. Lennie hopped up onto the slightly submerged platform that allowed George and his team to better study their subjects.

George stepped down onto the pool's ledge to inspect the animal. Lennie's skin was smooth and healthy. With a fish treat, a quick rub down, and a pat or two, he knelt down to look into Lennie's eye.

A chill swept down and grabbed his spine. Staring back at him were not the empty black eyes that he'd seen so many times. No, the eyes seemed deeper, almost physically sucking him in. There was a consciousness there, of something—no, *someone*—much more aware than himself, peering into his very soul.

He jerked back and shook his head. "George, you're a lonely man who should get out more," he mumbled to himself.

Lennie made a soft double-click and pushed away from the platform.

~*~

"Hello?" came a very sleepy voice over the phone.

"Patrick! Wake up and get your ass into the lab!" said George.

"Huh? What's wrong? Why are you yelling at me?" Patrick replied groggily.

"Besides it being ten o'clock and you're still in bed, something very weird is going on with Lennie and I need you down here right now to help me start running some tests."

"All right, all right. I'll be there in a few minutes. Keep your panties on."

Fortunately, Patrick lived in an apartment close by, but any hope that George might have of his student catching a shower and a shave before showing up was a bit of a lost cause, even on the good days.

Moments later a rather disheveled Patrick entered the pool area, parked his bike against the wall, and removed his backpack, asking, "Okay, what's up, Doc?"

Cute. Of all the grad students possible, he got the one making the Looney Tunes references.

George spent the next few minutes relaying the events of the morning. They talked about the testing options to see if they could characterize what exactly had changed with the whale and its altered brain functions.

"I think we should start with the same baseline tests we ran when we first assessed Lennie. That will give us something to compare apples-to-apples," suggested George.

"Then we could try teaching him some new words. You know, kind of like how you train parrots," offered Patrick. He'd recently entered the field of cetacean research so he didn't know much about anything, and George had to explain way more than he'd like, but he couldn't beat the price for the extra pair of hands. People weren't exactly beating down the door to study whale brains. He was a good kid, despite his shortcomings.

"While it might be interesting to see how Lennie would respond, I don't think it would go very far. See, the way orcas communicate, they use sounds in ways we don't understand. The sounds are densely packed, with complex patterns and frequencies. We've yet to be able to discern the language structure and thus any level of actual thoughts and intelligence—other than observing them. Their signals to each other are like you playing the recordings of five different overtures at the same time. It would sound largely unstructured and you wouldn't be able to determine the context of the different movements even if you could identify them.

"But that's only part of it. To make it even more difficult they also use sound to 'see' around them in the water depths. Sometimes their sounds only gather information about their environment, and are not to intentionally communicate with others in their pod."

"How do they see using sound? I'm mean I know about their sonar ability, but I don't really get it," said Patrick.

Be patient, he's learning all this for the first time, George reminded himself and took a deep breath.

"They use the sound that bounces back to not only measure how far away things are, but, to some degree, to see inside things or below the surface of the sea floor. Their brains then process this information in the augmented visual structures. So, from our perspective, they are 'seeing' with sound."

"Man, that's so cool!" replied Patrick.

"Exactly! It's like when dolphins can find things under the sand during the military tests. Or can use their sonar to detect the heartbeats of their prey. Or even know when humans in a boat above the water are freaking out because they are completely lost in the fog, and they lead the boat back to safety."

"Whoa!" exclaimed Patrick.

"So the way they collect and process information and communicate is much more parallel than we do. But if Lennie's behavior today is not just a coincidence, it means Lennie has just changed *everything*!"

There was confusion on Patrick's face. "I don't get it. How does Lennie change *anything*?"

George patiently explained how he was initially excited to have a defective whale brain so he could begin to understand the functioning version.

"But that was where I was wrong. I assumed Lennie had brain damage and the best I could hope for was to study an impaired specimen. But now that Lennie has tried to imitate my greeting, it proves that the higher cognitive functions are still in place, and the damage may be limited only to his equivalent speech centers."

"Okay, I'm lost again."

"Good grief, Patrick. Some days I'm surprised you're able to dress yourself!"

"Dude! Drop me a few breadcrumbs as to where you're going with this. I can tell you did the math, but you didn't show any of your work," the young man replied with some annoyance.

"Sorry, sorry. Look, what this means is meaningful communication with cetaceans and humans would be quite problematic because of the parallel nature of their communication and the speed at which they share information. Well, with Lennie, it now appears that process has been slowed down, but not destroyed in the injury. If that's true, then it might give a window into understanding their communication structure better and maybe even give us an opportunity to actually communicate with him beyond summersaults and fish treats!"

The flurry of activity by the two men in their planning and initial trials rivaled that of the days when they were working to save the animal's life. Yet this time Lennie seemed to understand what was going on and would float unnaturally still in the water for hours, chattering to himself as they ran their tests and collected their data.

~*~

Where might all this go if they were able to make a breakthrough in communication between their two species? A buzzing in George's pocket shook him from his inadvertent daydreaming. He dug his phone out from his pocket. Damn, it was Sharron, his ex-wife.

What does she want?

"Hello?"

"Hey, George. How's it going?"

She only cared how it was going when she wanted something. While he may have never actually understood her, some things were pretty obvious, even to him.

"Okay. What do you need, Sharron?"

"Oh, it's always straight to business with you, isn't it?"

There she goes.

"Sharron, why did you call?"

"Fine. Look, I need you to take Dillon for a few days."

Crap.

"This is not a good time for me—"

"I need you to watch him because… Look, George, I got remarried. His name is Mark. It all kind of happened really quick. My head's still spinning with everything, but Mark's a great guy and he's good with Dillon. I love him.

We're going to go on our honeymoon and I need you to watch Dillon while we're gone for a week."

For the briefest of moments, his peripheral vision washed out and a crushing black hole opened in his chest. Sitting down in a chair nearby, he struggled to breathe. Why was Sharron's marriage affecting him so? It wasn't like he was still in love with her, right? Was he? Denial? It was bound to happen sooner or later, but when it was 'later' it wasn't very...'now'.

"Hello? Heellooo?" He heard the faint voice coming from the phone he'd rested on his leg.

"Yeah, yeah, I'm here. When do you need me to watch him?"

"Well, we're kind of leaving in the morning for Hawaii..." Her words trailed off as his ears began to ring. Hawaii. That's where they'd gone for their honeymoon so many years ago. She truly was over-writing their life together.

"Fine. Bring him by my lab with his stuff and enough clothes for a week."

"Oh, thank you so much, George! This really means a—" He tapped the End Call button and put his phone to sleep. He didn't have the stomach to listen to her gratitude.

Moments later, there was a knock at the lab door. George opened it to find Sharron and Dillon standing there; her holding his suitcase and him grasping his stuffed dolphin, staring at his shoes.

"Wow!"

"What?" replied Sharron.

"You literally just called me. A little presumptuous, aren't you? There's no way—"

Sharron rolled her eyes and handed him a suitcase.

"Here. I'm sorry taking care of your son full-time for a week is soo inconvenient."

That was a low blow.

"This should be everything he'll need. We'll be back one week this Friday. Dillon, Mommy will miss you!" she said, gently putting her arm around him so as not to set him off into rocking back and forth. While he'd been to the lab on occasions, this was still a lot of change for him in one day. He didn't respond to her, but George could tell he understood everything that was going on by the simple fact Dillon wasn't looking through his Pokémon cards, which he tended to do habitually, and was listening to what was being said.

"Thanks again, George," she said. There was something different about her today...her perfume. It had always been his favorite, Sand and Sable, but for the first time since he met her, she'd changed it. Something sickly sweet smelling. The knot in his gut tightened as the reality of his failed marriage became more real. He held up a hand hoping she would stop talking, and turned, ushering Dillon to his office, leaving Sharron to close the door behind herself. Just like she did before with their relationship. There wasn't anything more to say.

George settled Dillon in his small office that contained an old wood desk each for him and a student along with just a small couch, which functioned as a bookshelf or as a bed as was the case for a while after Sharron asked for a divorce. For several weeks during that time, he only left the building to get some fast food or to buy something that he could make in the lounge microwave. Those were some dark nights. In hindsight, Lennie came along at just the right time to save him from himself.

He fetched a juice box and a chocolate bar from the building's vending machine for his son, as was their ritual when he visited the lab. When Dillon had finished his snack, George asked, "Dillon, would you like to get in the pool with my orca? It's just like a dolphin, but bigger and black and white instead of blue and grey."

Dillon sat flipping through his cards and didn't respond for what seemed like a minute when he stopped and slowly raised his hand This was his way of saying that it was okay and George could take him. Dillon had never looked him directly in the eyes or even smiled. George's heart ached having never had the smallest of connection with his child, when it came so readily and taken for granted by every other father. Truth be told, George was probably somewhere on the spectrum as well, making him a likely cause of Dillon's condition. Was his own disconnectedness with people somehow passed genetically to his son? Was his son given this lot in life because of him? These thoughts he tried to keep buried deep, but deep things always float back to the surface.

After dressing Dillon in a swimsuit George kept for him in the pool dressing room, he led his son over to the side of the pool to sit on the edge near the slightly submerged platform. Normally, George would never put his son in the pool with a wild orca, even though there have never been any reports of orcas attacking humans, but there was something different about Lennie. Sensing something was going on, Lennie swam over to observe and possibly get a fish out of it. George got in and moved Dillon over to sit on the edge of the submerged platform and dangled his legs over into the deeper water.

"Lennie, this is Dillon. You've seen him before. I thought it was time for the two of you to get better acquainted."

Lennie responded with an exhaled plum of warm spray.

"Dillon, lay back onto the platform and I'll help you float," said George after he had gotten fully into the pool. Dillon laid back with his eyes closed and arms crossed over his chest. Even though he'd never had a conversation with his son, at least Dillon trusted him.

"Okay, I'm going to float you over to Lennie and take your hand so that you can touch him. Is that okay?" By having him lay back into the water with eyes closed it would be similar to a sensory deprivation chamber which would be necessary in limiting the sensory overload to this new experience for his son. Dillon slightly raised one of his hands from his chest in agreement. George floated Dillon closer to Lennie who was watching almost curiously.

As George approached with Dillon, Lennie unexpectedly submerged, yet continued looking at the floating boy.

"What are you doing, Lennie? Are you suddenly shy?" asked George.

A sudden burst of subsonic sound waves emanated from Lennie, penetrating George's midsection like some misguided shiatsu massage, followed with rapid-fire clicks that could be heard above the surface and which reverberated up his spine. Lennie was effectively scanning Dillon. He'd never seen this level of intensity from the orca since it had been in his care.

"Lennie boy, what are you doing?" George said, gently slapping the surface of the water.

George looked at Dillon's face to see how he was reacting to all the noise, since his ears were mostly under the water line as he floated. A broad smile slowly spreads across his son's face.

Oh my God!

Tears welled in George's eyes. It was the first time since Dillon was a baby that he'd actually seen him smile!

Lennie, apparently satisfied with his inspection of the young man, surfaced and squeaked in his own unique excitement and swam away in a series of full barrel rolls.

Lennie, my friend, what are you up to?

~*~

As the days progressed, Dillon's time in the pool with Lennie increased, as did his son's smiles that filled George's heart with joy. Lennie seemed to be getting something out of it, too, in some way, and was more animated during the testing; almost as if he had a new friend. Before, George assumed Lennie's cognitive abilities had been disrupted to the point that companionship wouldn't mean anything to the whale. But the last week or so had proven him wrong. Could Lennie have been lonely all this time?

~*~

The hot water scalded his feet as George slipped into the burning embrace of a deep tub of bathwater. It had been years since he'd taken a hot bath as showers seemed more efficient. That had been his existence, avoiding life's irritations and chasing efficiencies at the cost of everyday, simple pleasures. But tonight, a hot bath was in order.

The testing with Lennie had gone well enough, but no breakthrough yet. He was missing something. At times, it almost seemed like Lennie was floating there waiting for him to figure it out. What could he be missing?

The thick hot air rose off the surface of the water and filled his lungs with each breath, his nose the last remaining part of his body just above the surface. In...out...in...out... he breathed in equal measure. Just as his shrink had taught him to help control his spells of anxiety. In…out…in…out…in…and his body was submerged in silence.

This must be what it has been like for Lennie. George had been forcing him to live in his own isolation, depriving him of the very elements natural to the whale. It had been just as unnatural to have the orca live in relative silence as it was for him at this moment, thirsting for any sound, any voice in the darkness.

Aware of the depleting oxygen, George surfaced for a renewed breath of hot, moist air and slipped beneath the water again. He had to get inside Lennie's head so he could figure out what he had been missing.

Slowly moving air from his lungs to the back of his throat George began to imitate the sounds of the deep ocean he'd spend half his life listening to. *Whooooooooamp, sqeeeeeeee, tick, tiiick, tick. Woooooooop, whiiiiiiii, tick, tick, tick, whooooooooo.* These were the voices of the deep water that had drawn him in to reveal their mystery so many years ago.

Another deep breath.

More calls. The sound echoed through the water, magnifying upon itself as his voice seemed to excite the natural frequency of the water that surrounded him. He could almost imagine these sounds bouncing around the tub, painting a picture of the middle-aged man lying there.

That was it!

George sat up within the tub suddenly, causing the water to slosh about and over the side, splashing onto the floor.

"Aaaahhh! Holy crap!" he screamed at the sight of a man leaning over the edge of the tub next to him.

"What do you want?" he called out, not able to see clearly with the hot water running over his eyes.

"Whoooooooooamp, sqeeeeeeee, tick, tiiick, tick," came the voice of the figure leaning so close.

George rubbed his eyes as he struggled to his feet, wiping his face with the towel hanging on a nearby rack.

"Dillon? What are you doing? Why are you in here? You're supposed to be in bed."

"Woooooooop, whiiiiiiii, tick, tick, tick, whoooooooo," came the reply as Dillon, his ear to the tub, held a toy orca in his hand.

George started laughing uncontrollably. Ungracefully, he got out of the tub, towel around his waist, and hugged his son. He had figured out what needed to be done. Both Lennie and Dillon already knew but didn't have the words to tell him.

~*~

The new sound database created by Patrick was the first step in an attempt to map Lennie's sounds to objects they presented to him. Surprisingly, Lennie was consistent with the vocalization he made for each object.

"Okay, George. I've hooked up a synthesized human voice to the computer. Now whenever Lennie names something that's in the database, we'll hear the translated word instead of us having to keep running back to the monitor to check," said Patrick.

"Good. Thanks," replied George. The boy was finally starting to come into his own, George mused.

George held up a fish.

Lennie squealed and clicked, followed a second later by a synthesized voice saying, "Fish."

The two men looked at each other.

"Yes!" they exclaimed in unison.

Next, a fresh squid. Again, Lennie responded with a sound and the computer voice said, "Squid." George and Patrick high-fived excitedly. Lennie seemed to catch on to this and made his own happy sound, dove into the pool, and resurfaced on the other side. He began making a new call, looking at something on that side of the room, and repeated the call several times.

"What does he want?" asked Patrick.

"I don't know. The computer doesn't recognize it either," George replied after glancing at the screen and turning to walk to where Lennie was indicating with his nose.

"Seriously, Lennie? There must be fifty things over here from diving gear to pool toys. Do you want to go through them one by one?" Patrick asked as he stared at the busy, rust specked grey wall.

"Well, unless you have a hot date waiting for you, we might as well."

"Funny, Doc. Reeeal funny."

"Good. Let's start with the pool toys."

Patrick brought a ball over to the side of the pool, and Lennie turned away slightly indicating no. The two of them went through several more items with no success. Patrick grabbed a set of diving rings and trudged back to poolside. Lennie squealed with happiness and repeated, several more times, the sound that initially brought them over.

"I'll be," George muttered. "Lennie's teaching us his vocabulary. Somehow he understands what we're doing."

"Wait a minute. A brain-damaged whale is teaching *us* now? When did that happen?"

With a backwards flip and a powerful stroke of his tail, which sprayed the two men with water, Lennie dove underwater and emerged a little further down the poolside.

"Hey, Lennie! Dude, was that really necessary?" exclaimed Patrick, mostly soaked from head to toe.

"He probably didn't appreciate you calling him 'brain damaged'," said George.

Lennie squealed with excitement and began repeatedly making a new sound as he looked at something on the opposite side of the pool.

The only thing over there was a boogie board.

George ran over, grabbed the board, and held it up. Lennie continued his call.

"Patrick, did you get it in the database?"

"Yep. We now have the orca word for boogie board. I can hear the comments when we present this at the next conference. 'Wow, that was money well spent. You guys figured out the orca word for boogie board!'" George laughed. Lennie squealed.

"Can he, like, understand us?" asked Patrick.

"I don't think so. I think he's just picking up that we're excited about the word-object connection that he's made and is feeding on the excitement. Orcas are emotional pack creatures like humans and canines, so this doesn't really surprise me. Dogs have the emotional maturity and intelligence of a 2 to 5-year-old child. We think orcas are a little above that. So, effectivity we have a six-ton toddler who just figured out how to make Mom and Dad laugh," said George.

"Cool. Hey, wait. I'm not Mom, am I?" asked Patrick.

"Well, all I'm saying is that it isn't me," George replied, laughing as he fed Lennie a fish and patted him on the head. It felt good to laugh again.

Lennie squealed and clicked.

Lennie, you're something else!

"Fish!" enunciated the synthetic voice from the other side of the pool.

George laughed again and said, "Okay, you can have another," and threw another at the large orca. Lennie swam over, and George reached over the edge and rubbed him on the head.

"I hope you can understand me, Lennie, because it's been nice to have someone to talk to who doesn't give me the stink eye when I don't pick up on their subtle cues. You get me." Lennie remained for a moment and then slipped beneath the water. If he kept progressing like this, they really should look into finding another orca to keep him company, even though he may never recover to the point of going back into the wild.

After packing up their gear and returning it to George's already cluttered office, he poured himself a cup of hours-old coffee.

Crap! Burned the coffee again.

"If this keeps up, you know we'll kind of reach the limit of our tools, right?" said Patrick, sitting on his desk.

"What do you mean?"

"Well, it's one thing if Lennie wants to play this 'Let's Name Everything in the World Game,' but for some reason I think it may be a bit more than that. There's something in his eyes today. I think he's trying to actually communicate," said Patrick.

"You saw it too, huh? Yeah, I was thinking the same thing." George leaned back in his desk chair and put his feet on the edge of his desk.

"If that's the case, then our database is not of much use to start constructing an actual translator. That's all way beyond me. We're just recording his sounds and mapping them to our words. We need something that can go the other direction and start adding structure. We're now in deep water, pardon the pun, in taking this to the next level," said Patrick.

"Hmmm," mused George, "I remember hearing about a friend of a friend that works at the University of

Washington who's a linguist researcher, translation theory expert or something. Her name was Letchworth, Linkwork...no, Lekworth. Yes, Samantha Lekworth. I'll try to get in touch with her and see if she's interested in coming over and meeting our chatty friend."

~*~

Samantha Lekworth walked into George's lab several weeks later and scanned the small office, visibly unimpressed. While only in her mid-thirties, she was one of the leading language researchers in the nation. George had contacted her to work on his orca project and while initially hesitant, she agreed to spend some time to see if there were any worthwhile possibilities. To help, George provided her with all the video and audio recordings of Lennie since he'd arrived.

"Good morning, Dr. Martin—"

"Please, call me George."

"Ah, okay. George," she said, smiling uncomfortably for a second. "I think I have, well I'm not sure what to call it, this is such uncharted territory—"

"Samantha, just come right out with it," George prodded with a smile. Her right eyebrow raised in equal and opposite measure to the corners of her mouth at his familiarity.

"Okay, well I think I may have made a startling discovery."

"Now you have my attention." George dropped his feet from his desk and replaced them with his elbows.

"Yes, well, I took all of your video recordings from your pool after the orca—"

"Lennie."

"Yes, when Lennie was 'in the clear' from his injuries and you started working with—"

"You're telling me you've already gone through over six months' worth of video in a couple of weeks?"

"Dr. Martin...uh, George, if we are going to work together would you please quit interrupting me! And yes, I have gone through all of them. Some people speed read, I speed listen, I guess you could say."

"Okay, sorry. Please go on."

"Yes, well, using state-of-the-art A.I. language processing software that I created on another project, I compared the sound recordings—the word database you began creating—and I believe I'm beginning to see the structure of his thoughts by the way he refers to things. Now that I have some basic structure, it's...possible to take the translation to the next level." Standing in front of George's desk, she rubbed the light band that remained on her finger where there once was a ring.

"You mean we could actually talk to Lennie?" asked Patrick from the doorway. Samantha jumped, evidently not hearing him arrive.

"Uh, yes. I think I can. Again, this has never been done before to any great success with any other species, let alone one that may be of equal intelligence to ourselves."

"Sweet!" exclaimed Patrick. George chuckled.

"This is where your expertise comes in, Doctor...uh, George. It might be possible to use the software to translate both ways. Can we use, what do you call them...a hydrophone as a speaker in the water, or should we just use one poolside? Can they hear out of the water?"

"Okay, one question at a time." He smiled as he raised his hand. "Hydrophones are microphones, so they won't work, but I have some underwater speakers that I helped design with a Japanese colleague several years ago. They have a low-frequency response sub-20 kilohertz sounds, which can be heard by humans, but also goes up to high-frequency sounds that we can't hear up to 150 kHz."

"Uh, okay. The other thing that I wanted to let you know is that I used some wavelet mathematics along with the recorded sounds from the orca—"

"Lennie," corrected Patrick this time.

"Lennie." Samantha shot him an irritated glance. "And I believe I can concur with your theory that the nature of the brain injury not only slowed down his communication centers, but also made his communication more serial like our own. And if this proves to be true, then it might be possible to take what we learn here and create a system that could pack our method of communicating into something that might be understandable to normal orcas."

In that moment, George noticed her, truly *noticed* her, for her brilliance and it was very attractive.

"What?" she asked.

"Hmm? What?" George replied.

"I don't know. I said we might be able to one day talk to normal orcas and you got this silly look on your face and just stared at me," said Samantha.

"Oh, don't mind him, he is kind of creepy, but in a lovable way," replied Patrick.

For the first time since he was a teenager, the telltale warm sensations of a blush washed across George's face.

"Uh, sorry. My mind just wandered there for a second. Gotta go…do…that thing I was going to do," he said as he quickly exited the small room.

~*~

"Okay George, it looks like Dr. Lekworth is ready and we're set up on our end. How about you?" Patrick asked as George walked into the pool area.

George entered the pool and Lennie swam over and hopped onto the pool platform. With a wave of his arm toward the beach ball on the opposite end of the pool, Lennie followed the motion but looked back as if studying him for a moment. With a heave of incredible muscle, the orca leapt into the pool, retrieved the ball, and squealed something as he nudged it toward George.

The trio looked toward the monitor to see the words being placed real-time. What would the computer algorithms piece together? Would the latest in machine learning produce brilliance or utter grammatical trash? Word by word was translated, including the reference to 'ball', but the algorithms were unable to identify the last two chunks of sound from Lennie.

"Hmmm, nothing much. Let's try it again with a different object to give the machine's learning algorithms more to work with," suggested Samantha.

"Okay. Patrick, throw in the noodle," called George.

"Go get the noodle," George commanded Lennie as he waved his arm in the object's direction.

Again, Lennie dove into the pool, retrieved the object, and issued a string of squeals and clicks, seemingly quite happy with himself. The computer searched for matches in the database and again the last two sounds were not identifiable, but they were the same as the last two sounds from the previous run. However, one of the words was identified as 'pool noodle'. This exercise was tried a few more times when the software popped-up a window with some additional information.

"Hold on guys, the translation AI has identified some possible meanings for the two unidentified sounds Lennie keeps making," said Samantha. "It's suggesting one word he's using for himself and the other is functionally used in a similar way as our verb 'to get'."

"Are you serious? So, the object is first followed by the personal pronoun and verb? Cool, Lennie talks like Yoda!" said Patrick.

"The software indicates that it's within 98% confidence. Those are pretty good betting odds," said Samantha, ignoring Patrick.

"Well done, Samantha," said George. She cast him a glare that dropped the temperature of the room.

"What? Seriously, we couldn't have gotten this far without you."

Her right eyebrow rose.

Not the eyebrow thing again. People really should come with a decoder ring.

They spent the following week going through deliberate activities designed by Samantha to try and drive out the subtler linguistic structures of the orca language and aid in creating the beginnings of a reliable software translator.

"Okay, I think we're at a place where I would like to run the first test to see if we can go from the object naming tests and on to actually having a conversation at some level with Lennie," Samantha announced during their morning pool-side tag-up meeting. Patrick had yet to make it in. "By the way, thanks for upgrading the coffee to drinkable."

"You're welcome. It's coming out of Patrick's semester stipend. Anyway, as far as I know, everything's good to go."

"Hey, wait! What was that about me paying for coffee?" said Patrick.

"Nice of you to join us this morning. Pour yourself a cup. I think there's a doughnut in my office from yesterday," said George.

"You spoil me, Doc."

George helped Dillon onto the submerged platform. Even though Sharron was back from her honeymoon, he tried to get Dillon into the pool with Lennie at least once a week as there definitely was some improvement in Dillon's responsiveness just by being around Lennie.

"Ready to lay back, Dillon?"

"Yeah," replied Dillon.

Goosebumps ran up George's arms. That one simple word still got him even though Dillon started saying it over a week ago. Maybe it was something like Dr. Temple Grandin, who was autistic, but who credited being around cattle for helping her to achieve what she had in life. It didn't matter, but what did was the fact that his son was now talking to him!

"Think the next round of tests will work?" George asked Samantha.

She shrugged. "Yes, no, who knows? I mean, nothing like this has ever been done. But then again, no team has ever had a willing subject like Lennie. I don't even know where to start verifying the accuracy of my human-to-orca translator...for God's sake we've never had a proper conversation with another species to even compare against! That is, if you don't consider my attempt to communicate with men."

"Funny. Very funny, Sam," George replied with the hint of a smile. She was funnier than he'd pegged her to be. "Okay, I guess if Lennie squirts water in our faces, we'll go back to the drawing board with the translator."

Lennie watched intently from the platform near Dillon. Seeming to sense the team was ready to start, he squealed, "Hello."

Patrick laughed and dropped the special speaker into the water. Lennie immediately released a series of squeaks and clicks that were translated into human voice as,

"Lennie want fish." They laughed and Patrick threw one in.

"I kind of miss the Yoda-speak, Dr. Lekworth. Can we have the software stop rearranging it?" asked Patrick.

Samantha laughed. "Maybe after we get the structure nailed down."

George said, "Lennie, can you understand me?"

The reply came as a series of squeals and clicks that sounded very orcaesque. The computer translated, "Yes."

"My name is George."

"Yes. George," came the translator's synthesized voice and Lennie let loose a squeal of happiness. The team was ear-to-ear with smiles.

For the first time in history we've broken the language barrier on the terms of the animal, learning their language, hearing their thoughts! All these years of work finally paying off! thought George.

"Lennie, are you happy here?"

"Yes, no. Like George."

'Like George'? Was he complimenting or commiserating?

"Why are you not happy?" asked George.

"Lennie miss family. Water is dark with no family."

"What do you mean dark without family?"

"When Lennie make sound to see in water, all family see. When Lennie talk, all family hear, same thoughts flow."

George blanched and turned off the microphone.

Oh no…

After a few uncomfortable moments Patrick asked, "What's wrong?"

"Orcas use echolocation to augment their eyesight to 'see' their world. And as a byproduct of living in a pod, they effectively eavesdrop off each other's echolocation waves and overhear the other pod members' conversations almost to the point of being a hive-like mentality. Lennie's voice is the only one illuminating his world in the pool right now and the *only* thoughts Lennie experienced since being here are his own, until now." George became more intense.

"It would be like growing up in a family of ten brothers and sisters, and sharing a bedroom, all of your toys, and being homeschooled together with your mother and father for your entire life. And then suddenly you're locked in a room with no lights, no sound, no windows, with only a flashlight, and alone with only your thoughts. Losing an individual is not as great of a loss to the pod, but it would be devastating to the individual. How could we have done this to these animals all these years?"

George slowly reached to turn on the microphone. "Lennie, I'm sorry you are sad. I hope you get to see your family again." The orca just stared at him. He lifted up a picture and the synthesized translator voice said "dolphin" when the orca squealed.

"Yes, this is a dolphin. We have seen orcas sound like dolphins when they are kept together. Can you understand dolphins?" Lennie didn't respond but looked at each of them before returning eye contact to George.

"Yes," came the reply. The team looked at each other in amazement. Becoming more excited George asked, "Do they have thoughts like you?"

"Yes. No. Dolphins' thoughts flow simple."

Patrick reached over and turned off the mic. "Why does he keep saying thoughts 'flow'?"

Samantha replied, "I believe it's an artifact of their perception of reality based upon how they interact with their environment. I suspect that's why Lennie uses the same idea for flow, swim, move, connect, think, etc."

Patrick nodded and turned the mic on again.

George continued, "We have seen some orcas eat dolphins. Why?"

Again, there was a long pause. "Not for food. For reminding dolphins of place in the water."

"I see. Why do you not eat George if George is in the water? You are bigger and stronger than George." He worded his sentence to help keep it simple for the translation software. Goodness knows what Lennie was actually hearing. Another pause, and unexpectedly Lennie launched off the platform and swam away silently.

"I guess that's all for today," said Samantha.

"Great! When the questions get hard, he up and runs," muttered Patrick.

"Well, let's pack things up," said George. No sooner had he made the comment, Lennie rushed back onto the platform surprising them all and nearly washing Dillon off the platform. Dillon! In all the excitement of conversing with Lennie, George had forgotten about him. Some father he was! A regular Father of the Year. But his son floated quietly on the pool platform with a grin on his face.

The translator came to life. "Thoughts had to flow. You look strange to orcas. Not like any fish or ones like family. In beginning, we curious. Dolphins still are. We watched you. We then understood you. You hunt fish. Fish do not hunt you. Some humans not hunt for food. You very like orcas."

The team looked at each other dumbfounded, amazed at the depth of understanding.

Lennie continued, "We see your body where thoughts flow. Not the same as orcas. Missing pieces. Orcas been in ocean for many cycles, not as many as voices from deep, but orca thoughts flow longer than humans'."

"Who are the voices from the deep?" asked George.

"Like orcas. Live in the deep and whose thoughts flow deeper than the water." Patrick looked to Samantha who held up her hands and shrugged.

Could it be...? George fumbled through some more charts and turned around one showing a blue whale. "Is this a voice from the deep?"

"Yes. One."

"You can understand them?"

"Small. Yes."

"And they have deep thoughts?"

"Yes. Their thoughts flow ways orcas not much understand. Even lights above the ocean have no hidden thought for voices from deep. One of their thoughts orcas understand now and orcas feel...sad for all like George."

"What do you mean 'sad for all like George'? Why?" asked George.

"The voices from deep say no tomorrow for all like George. The ocean will return as before."

A chill washed over George. His chest constricted. He struggled for breath. He struggled to calm the hammer pounding in his chest. Lennie had told him an unexpected yet undeniable truth.

Please God, no!

There was no doubt humans had wrecked the land and were polluting the oceans, but now the whales themselves were sealing man's fate.

"What do you mean?" George asked. Maybe, just maybe, this was just a 'lost in translation' thing.

Lennie rolled off the platform and oriented himself, submerged in the water, toward Dillon. With an intense string of sounds, Lennie directed the burst at the boy who, in turn, smiled, opened his eyes, and looked George in the eyes.

Not at his forehead, as Dillon had done in the past, but square in the eyes; soul to soul...and he was smiling! The world froze around them. Father and son. His son seeing him for the first time. His father and not just a caretaker. His heart, which had previously threatened to implode under Lennie's words, now strained under the swelling of love within. A reservoir of a lifetime of love waiting to break free, waiting to connect with his son. For the second time, he fell through the eyes of another. Another mind freed.

In the background of his mind, George was vaguely aware of the other two who prattled on about the system not being able to interpret what Lennie had communicated. But he knew.

Lennie lurched back up onto the platform, splashing father and son, dragging George back to the moment. Lennie squeaked and clicked another stream of sounds, pausing for the translation. "Dillon understand. Dillon important to future of those like George."

"Wait. What? No! What does Dillon have to with any of this?"

"George," a familiar male voice echoed in the large room.

Turning with a start, his old friend Tom Gladwell stood in the doorway flanked by two men dressed in uniforms.

"George, it appears we have a lot to talk about."

~*~

12 Things You Need to Know About Merfolk

Philip Harris

~*~

We all know the lovable, family friendly mermaids of film and television but merfolk are a very real threat to your safety. As more disturbing details of the events at the Atlantis One construction site come to light and public interest in these mysterious creatures grows, we've put together a brief guide to all things merfolk.

1) The first known merfolk stories appeared in Assyria around 1000 BC but archaeologists working at the Marianas Trench survey site have discovered artifacts that indicate merfolk formed complex social and political structures at least three thousand years before that. Cities with as many as thirty thousand inhabitants are thought to have existed at the height of the Eighth Dynasty—a period of time that corresponds with 3000-1000 BC.

2) Although there were many unconfirmed sightings of merfolk over the centuries, it wasn't until the mid 1800s that truly credible witnesses spoke of their experiences. Even then, reports of "watery she demons" and "foul fish men" were dismissed by most people. It took anthropologist Abigail Kiernan's ground-breaking research into the "sea people" to really put the merfolk on the map.

3) The sea people moniker remained in common use until the 1862 publication of Kiernan's book, *Undersea: The Life and Habits of Mere-folk in the English Channel.* Dissatisfied with the "unjust anonymity" of the sea people, she named them mere-folk after the Old English word for sea. Over the years, usage of the name has changed and now merfolk has become the accepted form.

4) Three years after the publication of her book, Kiernan's research came to a dramatic end when she vanished somewhere along the coast of the Isle of Wight, a small island located four miles off the coast of southern England. Her boat was found drifting two miles offshore. Her belongings—a coat, life jacket, water, food, flashlight and her notebook—were still in the boat. There were no signs of a struggle and her disappearance remains a mystery. Many believe she was killed by the very race she was studying and that this is the earliest known case of a merfolk attack. Others take a more fanciful view. They believe she chose to join the merfolk and cite her discarded coat and life jacket as proof.

5) Whether or not Abigail Kiernan was killed by merfolk, there is no doubt when the merfolk uprising began. On the morning of February 3rd, 1931, the

inhabitants of the Isle of Wight woke to find themselves under attack. An unknown number of merfolk came onshore and systematically killed most of the 98,000 inhabitants. Two hundred men, women and children are thought to have escaped the island using fishing boats and, most famously, a makeshift raft built from household furniture. But their freedom was short lived. The merfolk, giving chase across the English Channel, hunted down and overwhelmed all but two of the craft.

6) The eight survivors of the Isle of Wight massacre— the Tomlinson family and Mary and Alec Wolfe—played a crucial role in the early days of the "War of the Waves" that followed. Their eyewitness accounts of the attack enabled the British Army and Navy to successfully defend Britain's shores against the merfolk incursion. Justine Tomlinson, the last known survivor of the massacre, died in Oxford in July 2007 at the ripe old age of 77.

7) Outnumbered and outgunned, the merfolk resorted to guerrilla tactics. Nighttime raids of coastal and riverside towns were frequent occurrences and the Water Defence Volunteers or "Water Watch" became a fixture in towns and villages all across England. Nine months after the start of the war, the British Navy began bombarding the merfolk's underwater cities with specially modified depth charges. Within weeks, the merfolk had been forced to abandon their homes and flee to deeper waters. The War of the Waves was over. W-Day is now celebrated across Britain on the 2nd Sunday of January.

8) The International Ocean Defence Force was formed in February 1932, exactly one year after the merfolk attack on the Isle of Wight, and has been

protecting humans from merfolk ever since. IODF define and patrol the "no-sail" zones around known merfolk locations, investigate and track merfolk sightings and attacks, and provide educational courses on the dangers of merfolk to schools and colleges around the world.

9) In 2014, the commander of IODF, General Jonathan Green, came under criticism over the increased number of merfolk attacks outside of the no-sail zones. Citing budget cuts and lowered public vigilance as the cause of these incidents, General Green vowed to "take back our oceans" and "expel the merfolk menace" once and for all. His controversial proposal, known as Project Saltwater, was approved by the United Nations in June 2015.

10) Despite extensive protests, construction of the first stage of Project Saltwater, the nuclear powered underwater base known as Atlantis One, began on March 6th, 2016. Costing an estimated 732 billion dollars to build, the base will be home to over five thousand servicemen and women, fifteen Virginia class submarines, and almost two hundred support and reconnaissance vehicles.

11) Since construction of Atlantis One began, there have been sixteen major accidents. The most recent occurred when a deep-sea excavator collided with a transport submarine carrying fifty workers to the dig site. The workers and the five crew manning the excavator were killed, bringing the total confirmed deaths at the site to 219. The cause of the collision has not been confirmed.

12) Despite the increasingly frequent accidents and widespread concerns for workers' safety, spokespersons from the IODF have confirmed that Atlantis One is still on track to be completed in October 2019, at which time, it will become the defence force's base of operations and the key to ridding the world of the merfolk menace, once and for all. Until then, the IODF recommends extreme caution when travelling outside of the designated "green water" routes.

~*~

The Lost Tapes–Sirens of Bartholomew

Daniel Arthur Smith

~*~

"RECORDING BEGINS WITH TODAY'S DATE, JULY 29ᵀᴴ 2017. My name is Agent Melissa Muldoon. Present with me is Agent Lawrence Meyer. Commencing interview of one Vasyli Volkov, sole survivor of the Russian deep-water research vessel Anatoly Brunov. *Mister Volkov has agreed to share information concerning the disappearance of the* Brunov's *crew. Though Mister Volkov is a Russian citizen, he speaks English, so we have no need for a translator. Mister Volkov could you—"*

"I have dual citizenship."

"Excuse me?"

"You mentioned, for the recording, that I was a Russian citizen."

"Are you not?"

"I am. But I'm also an American citizen. My parents were diplomats. I was born and raised in Virginia."

"And that's why you don't have an accent."

"Correct."

"For the record. Mister Volkov is both a Russian and American citizen and speaks native English"

"Thank you."

"Moving on. Please state your name and age."

"Vasyli Volkov. 22."

"Excellent. Mister Volkov, two days ago the fishing vessel Nautica Vale *discovered the* Brunov *adrift 50 kilometers south of Bermuda."*

"Yes. That is correct."

"The Brunov *has a crew manifest of 23. The captain of the* Vale *reported that when they boarded the* Brunov, *you were the only one aboard. Locked in the ship's pantry. From the outside. Is that true?"*

"Yes. I was in that hold for three days. Fortunately, I was locked in with food and water."

"I'd say very fortunate. Yet your hands are bandaged. The medical reports state that you broke bones in your hands and that your fingers had open sores."

"I was trying to get out."

"Of course. Can you please tell us how you came about being locked in the pantry?"

"I was locked in by my uncle."

"His name?"

"Peter Malikova. My mother's brother."

"Here he is. The manifest states he is the Brunov's cook."

"Yes. My parents sent me to work for him. I had some trouble in school.

"Which school was that?

"Georgetown."

"The Hoyas. Agent Meyer here went to Georgetown. That's a good school. Quite a jump to a galley."

"Like I said, I had some trouble."

"*What kind of trouble?*"

"I lost my scholarship."

"*Ah. So you were sent to work with Uncle Peter.*"

"That's right."

"*So why did uncle Peter lock you in the pantry? And, where is he now?*"

"They took him."

"*They? Who is 'they'?*"

"The Rusalka. That's what he called them. We were answering a distress beacon. When my uncle recognized what was happening, he locked me in the pantry."

"*And who are the Rusalka? Terrorists?*"

"No. Rusalka means mermaid. Sort of."

"*Terrorists who call themselves mermaids?*"

"Not terrorists. Not mermaids either, exactly. Sirens."

"*You were boarded by sirens? Singing women? Mister Volkov, are you currently prescribed psychotropic pharmaceuticals?*"

"No."

"*To your knowledge did you consume any psychedelics?*"

"I know it sounds crazy. When I was first told of the Sirens, I laughed. '*Sirenas de Bartolomé*' is what Santayana called them."

"*Fernando Santayana y Miranda, the engineer?*"

"Yeah. The old Spaniard called them that, right before he crossed himself."

"*Okay. From the beginning.*"

"We'd been out there for weeks."

"*Doing what?*"

"I don't know. A whole lot of nothing. I mean, I spent most of my time in galley and the mess."

"*So you have no idea?*"

"Well. They have those subs. Two of them. Viktor told me they were mapping the sea floor, volcanic formations, stuff like that."

"*Viktor?*"

"He's a tech. Nice guy. The only guy on the *Brunov* I could really relate to. He has a ton of cool video games. When we weren't on duty, that's what we did. A lot of Call of Duty.

That's what we were playing when the storm hit."

"Storm?"

"From out of nowhere. The mate was pissed. He came in screaming at us to get to stations. So I went back to the galley. Alarms were going off. People were scrambling to pull their vests on. I asked one of the scientists what was going on. He told me they'd found something and to get my gear. It was the first time I felt the *Brunov* rock."

"Rock?"

"It was like the ship was being picked up and shaken. I'd never felt rough water. It was like being on a roller coaster. You know how your belly gets all butterfly? I couldn't see outside but my stomach was telling me that we were rising and falling. Then it all just stopped, and everything went green."

"What do you mean, everything went green?"

"Everything went green. I thought the lights all had some kind of filters on them, because even the flashing alarm lights went from red to green. But then, went I got to the galley, Santayana and my Uncle were at the window. And the outside was the same shade of green. The sky was green, the ocean was glowing fluorescent green. Like a glow stick. That's when Santayana first started talking fast and crossing himself."

"What was he saying?"

"I don't speak Spanish, but I think it was some kind of prayer because I heard him repeat Maria every time he crossed himself."

"A glowing sea is not uncommon. It's caused by bioluminescent phytoplankton. I saw it from a catamaran in the Bahamas. The microorganisms emit light in response to stress. The storm must have stressed an algae bloom and the sky reflected the iridescence."

"Maybe. I'm not a scientist. And maybe that's what produced the green mist."

"Green mist?"

"Yeah. A green mist. It drifted down past the window. Then we noticed it creeping into the galley. That's when the Spaniard said the Sirens were coming and my uncle locked me in hold. I was screaming for him stop. I heard them singing even before the latch was locked. I wanted out. But it was too late."

"The singing?"

"Yes. It was beautiful. Ethereal. They were angels. I'd never heard anything like it before. I was exhilarated. I never felt so alive. When they came, I begged to go with them. I beat on the door but I couldn't budge it."

"You saw them?"

"Yes. Through the window of the pantry door. I saw one. She sang so beautifully."

"You mentioned that. What did she look like? What nationality?"

"Nationality? She wasn't even human. I mean, she had two legs and two arms, but her hands and feet were clawed and webbed, and her body was spotted, like a leopard, and she had the head of a cuttlefish, with a number of squiggly arms surrounding her mouth and thin rift fins running along the sides that rippled as she sang. I banged as hard as I could to get her attention. She turned toward me. Her W-shaped eyelids spread open and her large black pupils fixed on me. I thought she was going to free me. To take me with her. But she left without me. Just faded away."

"You're insinuating you were boarded and the crew taken by mermaids?

"I'm not insinuating anything. I'm telling you it was singing sirens that lured the crew. I saw it myself. And they would have taken me, too, had I not been locked in."

"I see. Mister Volkov, we're going to get some help for you. You've obviously been traumatized by this experience. What you're describing—"

"Listen. I can help you find the others. We just need to go back."

"Rescue helicopters are searching a 500-square mile area, Mister Volkov, and plans are underway to extend the search. I assure you we're doing all we can."

"I have to go back. You don't understand. I have to. I can't bear it."

"Mister Volkov, you're a young man. What you're experiencing is survivor's guilt. I told you. We're doing everything we can to find your crew

mates."

"No. It's not that. I have to go back. I have to escape it."

"Escape what, Mister Volkov? You escaped whatever fate they faced."

"Can't you hear them? The sirens of Bartholomew. It's so sweet."

"Hear what? I don't hear any song."

"Oh, I escaped the siren's song, but I can't escape their silence."

~*~

ABOUT THE AUTHORS

Kevin Lauderdale has written essays and articles for the *Los Angeles Times*, *The Dictionary of American Biography*, and **McSweeneys.net**. His short fiction has appeared in several of Pocket Books' *Star Trek* anthologies as well as various small press publications. His story "Box 27" was published in the science journal *Nature*. This is his fourth appearance in Canyons of the Damned. He hosts the Old Time Radio podcast, "*Presenting the Transcription Feature*," and co-hosts "*Temple of Bad*," the podcast about movies that are so bad, they're practically a religious experience, both on the Chronic Rift network. He is a member of SFWA and HWA.

For more information, visit
kevinlauderale.livejournal.com

Terry R. Hill, a Texas native, was trained with two degrees in aerospace engineering. He has worked for NASA since 1997 with a very satisfying career as an engineer and project manager spanning programs from the international space station's navigation software, to next generation space suit design, to exploration mission planning, to mitigating the health effects of space on astronauts. While supporting the manned space program has been a lifetime passion, writing of different worlds, alternate futures and the human condition has filled his spare time.

For more information, visit terryrhill.net

Philip Harris was born in England but now lives in Canada where he works for a large video game developer. Not content with creating imaginary worlds for a living, he spends his spare time indulging his love of writing. His published books include **The Girl in the City Trilogy** and an homage to the old pulp science fiction serials - **Glitch Mitchell** and the **Unseen Planet**.

His short fiction has appeared in numerous anthologies and magazines including **The Jurassic Chronicles, Bones, Uncommon Minds, The Anthology of European SF**, and **Peeping Tom**. He has also worked as security for Darth Vader.

For more information, visit solitarymindset.com

Daniel Arthur Smith is the author of the international bestsellers *Hugh Howey Lives*, *The Cathari Treasure*, *The Somali Deception*, and a few other novels and short stories. He also curates the phenomenal short fiction series *Tales from the Canyons of the Damned*.

He was raised in Michigan and graduated from Western Michigan University where he studied philosophy, with focus on cognitive science, meta-physics, and comparative religion. He began his career as a bartender, barista, poetry house proprietor, teacher, and then became a technologist and futurist for the Fortune 100 across the Americas and Europe.

Daniel has traveled to over 300 cities in 22 countries, residing in Los Angeles, Kalamazoo, Prague, Crete, and now writes in Manhattan where he lives with his wife and young sons.

For more information, visit danielarthursmith.com

~*~